P9-CQH-813

The Worst Name in Third Grade

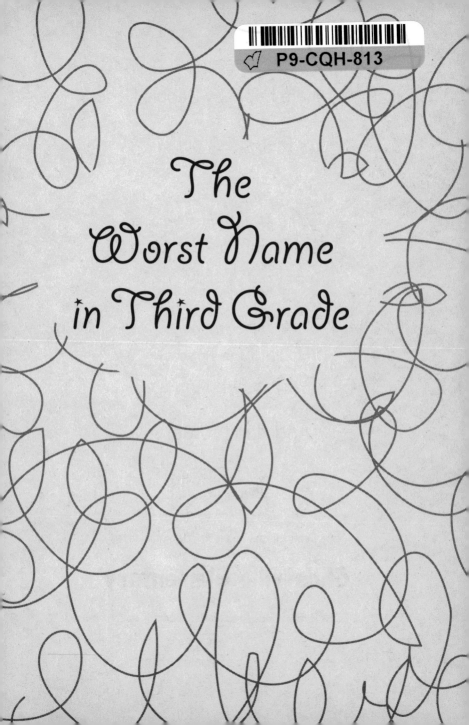

Want more books by Debbie Dadey?

Then check out . . .

Swamp Monster in Third Grade
Swamp Monster in Third Grade #2:
Lizards in the Lunch Line

The Slime Wars
Slime Time

with her son Nathan Dadey

And don't forget . . .

by Debbie Dadey and Marcia Thornton Jones

Ghostville Elementary®

by Debbie Dadey and Marcia Thornton Jones

The Worst Name in Third Grade

by Debbie Dadey
illustrated by Tamara Petrosino

SCHOLASTIC INC.
New York   Toronto   London   Auckland   Sydney
Mexico City   New Delhi   Hong Kong   Buenos Aires

If you purchased this book without a cover, you should be aware
that this book is stolen property. It was reported as "unsold and destroyed"
to the publisher, and neither the author nor the publisher has
received any payment for this "stripped book."

No part of this publication may be reproduced, stored in a
retrieval system, or transmitted in any form or by any means, electronic,
mechanical, photocopying, recording, or otherwise, without written
permission of the publisher. For information regarding permission, write to
Scholastic Inc., Attention: Permissions Department, 557 Broadway, New York, NY 10012.

ISBN-13: 978-0-439-72000-7
ISBN-10: 0-439-72000-1

Text copyright © 2005 by Debra S. Dadey
Illustrations copyright © 2005 by Scholastic Inc.
SCHOLASTIC, LITTLE APPLE, and associated logos are
trademarks and/or registered trademarks of Scholastic Inc.

12 11 10 9 8 7 6   7 8 9 10 11 12/0

Printed in the U.S.A.   40
This edition first printing, June 2007

For my beautiful niece Amanda
and her new husband, Nicholas—
best wishes for a happy marriage
—D.D.

Contents

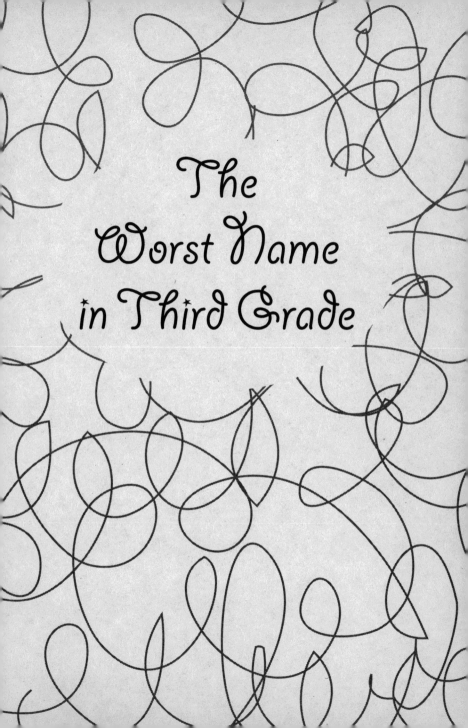

The
Worst Name
in Third Grade

1

The Best

My name is Bridgett, which isn't so bad. My last name is Butt, and that's bad. Kids always laugh at it. Only one red-haired kid never laughed at my name. That's why Amanda Reynolds is my best friend. We've been buddies ever since kindergarten.

Now we're in third grade and our teacher is the best teacher in the whole world. She's the only teacher who didn't giggle when she said my name for the first time. Not even a little bit. Maybe it's because her own name is a little different. Her name is Mrs. Holiday, like all the

1

really great days in a year rolled into one special person. She didn't give us presents every day, but she sometimes did give us stickers and even a couple of parties for good behavior.

"I love Mrs. Holiday," Amanda said one morning when we got off the school bus. "She's the only teacher who lets kids have snacks and water bottles at their desks."

"We are soooo lucky," I told Amanda after I took the gum out of my mouth. I always chew gum on the bus. Don't tell anyone, but I used to suck my thumb. I don't anymore, no matter what my dumb big brother, Tom, says. Anyway, my mom taught me to chew gum on the bus so the kids wouldn't laugh at me for sucking my thumb. Instead, they laugh at me because my last name is Butt. I'm not sure that's any better.

On my way into school, Mikey Parsons from our class walked by me and gave me a little nudge. "Hey, Butt-head."

My face turned bright red, but Amanda didn't waste a minute. She sang, "Girls go to college to get more knowledge, boys go to Jupiter to get more stupider."

I smiled, but Mikey didn't seem to care. He just stuck his tongue out and walked away.

"I feel soooo sorry for the other kids in third grade," Amanda said, ignoring Mikey and heading toward the front door. Buses unloaded all around us. It was like Grand Central School Station.

I pulled the heavy school door open for Amanda and we went into the crowded hallway. "It must be awful to have Mrs. Baker or Miss Cook for a teacher," Amanda said. "I hear they're not half as good as Mrs. Holiday."

I nodded and put my gum back in its wrapper. Fifth Street School didn't allow gum chewing. I would save it for the bus ride home so I didn't have to waste another piece. I don't mind ABC (Already Been Chewed) gum as long as it's mine. "I wish we could be in third grade forever and ever," I said.

"And always have Mrs. Holiday for our teacher," Amanda added.

I figured I was pretty lucky. I might have the worst name in the world, but I did have the best best friend and the best teacher ever. And that was enough for me. What I didn't know was that all that was about to change.

2

Lovely

"You ladies look lovely today," Mrs. Holiday told me and Amanda as we walked into the classroom. That's one of the neat things about our teacher. She's always saying nice stuff like that. Some teachers just say, "Get in your seats," or "Be quiet," but our teacher says lovely things.

I smiled really big and said, "You look lovely, too." And she did. Mrs. Holiday had on a dress the color of orange sherbet. It sounds weird, but it looked beautiful on her. In fact, it looked lovely.

After we were all seated—even Mikey Parsons, who always took the longest to settle down—Mrs. Holiday stood up at the front of the room. "I have an announcement to make," she said.

That was very strange. Mrs. Holiday always took attendance and collected lunch money first. She never told us something first. An "announcement" sounded really important. Even Mikey Parsons sat up straight to see what was going to happen next.

"I would rather wait and tell you this later, but I don't want you to find out from someone else," Mrs. Holiday continued.

Find out *what* from someone else? I looked at Amanda. We both shrugged at the same time. That's one of the things I like best about Amanda—we always know when to shrug at the same time. That's how it is with best best friends.

"I have some rather sad news," Mrs. Holiday said. She had her hands out in front of her, and she twisted them together

like a pretzel. She was a tan pretzel with orange icing. "My husband found a new job in Texas, and we are moving in two weeks."

The words hit me like a fast-moving skateboard. I couldn't breathe. I couldn't talk. Everything got blurry.

"Please don't go!" Amanda cried out.

Mrs. Holiday smiled her lovely smile. "I'm sorry, but I love my husband and must move with him. You will have a wonderful new teacher. Her name is Miss Snotgrass."

Several kids giggled when Mrs. Holiday said "Snotgrass," but Mikey laughed out loud. "Now, students," Mrs. Holiday said, "I hope you will be kind to your new teacher and give her a chance to get to know you all. I know it will be hard to change teachers in the middle of the school year, but I also know that you can do it. Miss Snotgrass is a lovely person."

I stared at Mrs. Holiday. Suddenly, her

orange dress was very, very ugly. In fact, it looked like a rotten pumpkin. Just a few minutes ago, everything had been lovely, but now I had the feeling that nothing would ever be lovely again.

3

Mad

"Hey, rump roast!" someone yelled through the bus window as the door closed behind me. I gritted my teeth and kept on walking home, but I truly would have liked to kick Mikey Parsons in *his* rump. I just *knew* it was Mikey Parsons who had yelled.

So I was in a bad mood when I got home. My dumb big brother didn't help any. My parents divorced two years ago, and Mom works late on Tuesdays, so guess who babysits for me? That's right, my dumb eighth-grade brother, Tom. I don't think watching TV and eating popcorn should be called babysitting. He never lets me see the shows that I wanted to watch. I have to go up to my room to avoid being creeped out by all of his weird alien shows. Those are Tom's favorites.

"Hey, squirt," Tom yelled from the family room as I stomped into the kitchen. Our kitchen and family room are really just one big room. "You want to watch *Space Blood* with me?"

"No thanks," I grumbled, grabbing some popcorn out of his bowl as I walked past.

"Hey!" Tom said. "Get your own."

I dribbled popcorn out of my mouth just to make him mad. I knew that he'd have to clean it up or Mom would fuss. After all, I wasn't old enough to make popcorn (at least according to my mom). So if there was popcorn all over the carpet, then it would be Tom's fault.

My old dog, Bobo, hobbled over and tried to eat the popcorn off the carpet. "No, Bobo," I said. "You know that popcorn makes you sick." His big brown eyes peeked out from under his fluffy gray hair. Bobo's the oldest mutt in the history of the world. He's even older than the pyramids, I think. Bobo moves pretty slowly, so I scooped him into my arms and carried him up the stairs to my room. It's a good thing he only weighs about ten pounds.

"Bobo," I asked him, "what am I going to do? Mrs. Holiday is leaving."

We sprawled out on my green bedspread. Green is my new favorite color. I chewed my last piece of popcorn and sighed. Bobo looked at me with those sad brown eyes and licked my hand. He felt sorry for me. I felt sorry for me, too. I hugged Bobo. I knew he would understand. "I'm so glad you're my dog," I said. "At least you won't leave me like Mrs. Holiday."

Just thinking of Mrs. Holiday leaving made me feel so bad that I laid my head on my bed and sobbed. Now, normally

I'm not a crybaby, but this was terrible. The best teacher in the world was leaving, and we were getting a new teacher who probably hated kids.

I knew one thing for sure: There was no way I would ever like Miss Snotgrass. She had another thing coming if she thought she could teach me anything. I would show her.

4

Miss Snotgrass

I cried. Amanda cried. But it didn't matter. Mrs. Holiday left and Miss Snotgrass came.

Mrs. Holiday had moved away and we'd had our new teacher for almost one full day. The minute I looked at Miss Snotgrass, I decided that I didn't like her. Her teeth were too big and she smiled too much. If that wasn't bad enough, she gave us homework, too!

"She's nice," Amanda said with a giggle.

"She's mean," I snapped at Amanda. How could Amanda say that Miss

16

Snotgrass was nice? She had taken Mrs. Holiday's place, and that made Miss Snotgrass awful.

Amanda looked at me. We were on the monkey bars at recess. The monkey bars are the place to be when you're in third grade. I usually loved swinging upside down with Amanda, but today I suddenly didn't feel like swinging. I felt like being alone.

I hopped off the monkey bars and walked away. "Hey!" Amanda yelled. "Where are you going?"

Amanda and I always did everything together at recess, so I don't know why I didn't answer her. I think it had something to do with her liking Miss Snotgrass. It was like Amanda was being a traitor to Mrs. Holiday. And me.

We have this nature area on our playground that's filled with lots of trees and bushes. It's a great place to hide and think, so that's where I went. I sat down on a bench to think and think and think. I

didn't have any gum with me, so I chewed my lip instead. Lips aren't as tasty as gum, but they're always there when you need them.

"How could Amanda Reynolds like Miss Snotgrass?" I said out loud. A little robin flew by, but it didn't answer me. I looked all around at the pine trees and bushes. They didn't answer, either. A wasp buzzed around my face, but I swatted at it. Yikes!

The bell rang to end recess, so I trudged back toward the school building. I was alone, but Amanda wasn't. She was walking with Carey Armstrong! My best friend was walking with someone else! How could this be happening?

I marched up to Amanda. "Hey, why aren't you walking with me?" I asked her.

Amanda shrugged. "You left, so I started playing with Carey. And guess what?"

"What?" I asked with a terrible feeling in my stomach.

"Carey likes Miss Snotgrass, too," Amanda said.

Carey smiled, showing the big gap between her two front teeth. "I think Miss Snotgrass is beautiful," Carey said. "And Miss Snotgrass is even nicer than Mrs. Holiday."

I stared in horror. How could she say that? I waited for Amanda to set Carey straight. Amanda would tell her that no one was as good as Mrs. Holiday. But Amanda didn't say anything. She just nodded and followed Carey into the classroom.

It felt like the end of the world. Mrs. Holiday was gone, and so was Amanda. They had both left me. I figured things couldn't get any worse.

I was wrong.

5

Postcards from Texas

"Bridgett, would you please show the class where Africa is on the map?" Miss Snotgrass asked me in her funny, kind-of-southern accent.

She asked in a nice way, but I wasn't feeling nice. I looked over at Amanda and Carey. They were passing a note back and forth and giggling. I had this terrible feeling that they were giggling about me. I was so mad about everything that I snapped at Miss Snotgrass.

"No!"

Miss Snotgrass raised her skinny little eyebrows and asked, "Excuse me?"

I heard Amanda giggle again and I stood up next to my chair. "You're not my teacher, and I don't have to do what you say."

Nobody said a word, and Amanda definitely did not giggle. Miss Snotgrass just looked at me. Her eyes looked a little watery. I didn't know what else to do, so I ran. "I have to go to the bathroom," I blurted as I sprinted out the door.

In the bathroom, I paced back and forth. "Now what am I going to do?" I wondered out loud. I had yelled at a teacher. Kids got sent to the principal for things like that. Mr. Webster, our principal, would not feel sorry for me. He wouldn't care that Mrs. Holiday was gone. He would probably give me an awful punishment. What a horrible mess!

For a second, I pretended that my mom would let us move to Texas so I could be

in Mrs. Holiday's new class. "Oh, Bridgett, I missed you terribly," she would say. "I dreamed that you would move here." Of course, I would be the teacher's pet because she would know me the best. I would send postcards from Texas to Amanda that said, "I still have the best teacher ever, and you have Miss Snotgrass. Ha, ha."

That made me feel a little bit better, but when the bathroom door opened, I froze. It was Miss Snotgrass.

"Hello, Bridgett," she said softly. "Are you feeling okay?"

That was it! My way out of trouble! "No," I said quickly. "I'm feeling kind of funny."

"Oh, I'm so sorry," she said softly. "Let's get you to the nurse's office."

I went to the nurse's office with Miss Snotgrass, but I didn't like it. I didn't like anything about her. I just didn't know what to do about it.

6

Sick

"No," I groaned. How could the nurse send me back to class? I felt terrible.

"No temperature, back to class," Miss Feakes said with an evil smile. If she was even a little bit nice, she would have let me suffer on the nurse's cot until the bell rang, but she was mean through and through.

That's how I ended up back in the classroom with my head down on my desk. Mikey Parsons punched my arm as he walked by. "Let's see the Butt-girl hurl," he whispered. I looked up and saw him smirk as he walked away.

I just groaned and buried my head in my hands, but not before I saw Carey Armstrong giggle. What kind of person would laugh when someone else was sick and being made fun of? I knew the answer to that: the same kind of person who would like Miss Snotgrass.

Okay, so I really wasn't sick like I needed a doctor. I *did* feel horrible, though. Maybe if I closed my eyes, everything would go back to the way it used to be. I squeezed my eyes shut and tapped my heels together, just in case it would work like in *The Wizard of Oz*. I didn't have ruby slippers like Dorothy, but my tennis shoes were bright purple. Maybe that was close enough. One. Two. Three.

I popped open my eyes. Had things changed back? No. Miss Snotgrass still smiled in the front of the classroom. Her big front teeth made her look like a chipmunk. She saw me looking at her and she smiled even bigger, but I quickly ducked my head back into my arms.

I felt so bad that I barely made it to the bus in time. When I got there, all the good seats were taken. Amanda was sitting with Carey. I felt like crying. Amanda and I always sat together.

I walked past Amanda and Carey. They didn't even see me. Their heads were bent over and they didn't look up. They were too busy whispering. That's when I noticed that even the bad seats were taken. In fact, only one seat was left—the one right next to Mikey Parsons.

I gulped and did what I had to do. I sat down. Mikey didn't waste any time. He started teasing me right away. "Oh, yuck! I'm sitting next to Poopy Patty," he said loud enough for half the bus to hear.

"My name is NOT Poopy Patty," I snapped.

27

Mikey put his hand over his heart, at least where his heart would be if he had one. "Sorry, your name is Hilda Hiney, isn't it?"

"Mikey, you know my name. Why do you have to be so mean about it?" I asked, but then I didn't give him a chance to answer. "How would you feel if your name was Mikey Mudd? Or Peter Puke? Or Sam Slime?"

Mikey ignored my questions, but he did lean over and whisper in my ear, "How would you feel if your last name was Snotgrass?"

7

Bridgett Bad Mood

My name should have been Bridgett Bad Mood, because that's exactly how I felt when I got home that afternoon. Mom tried to cheer me up, but it didn't work. "Hello, honey," she said, giving me a hug at the door. "How was school?"

"Fine," I said before dropping my lunch box and bolting up the stairs. I didn't tell my mom how terrible things were because I didn't feel like talking about it, except to Bobo. But where was he?

"Bobo?" I called. "Come here, boy!"

Because Bobo is old, it usually takes him a few minutes to find me after I get home, but this time he wasn't around at all.

"Mo-o-o-om!" I yelled. "Where is Bobo?"

"He's in the laundry room," Mom yelled. "He's been acting funny today."

I walked into the laundry room and looked around. No Bobo. "Bobo?" I asked, peeking around a pile of dirty clothes. Bobo was lying with his head on a crumpled towel.

Bobo barked and gave me a lick on the nose. "Hello, boy," I said, scooping him into my arms. He groaned when I picked him up, but I know he was happy to see me because his tail slapped against my leg as I carried him upstairs.

"Oh, Bobo," I said when my door was safely shut. "The most terrible things happened today." Bobo listened and snuggled close on my bed while I told him my sad story.

For some reason, I got tears in my eyes when I was telling him about Mikey. "He teases me all the time," I sobbed. "Why is he so mean?"

Just then my bedroom door swung open. My big brother filled the doorway. "Who's being mean to you?" he asked, frowning.

I was so surprised to see Tom that I told him the truth. "Mikey Parsons teases me about my last name." I sniffled and wiped at my tears with the back of my hand.

Tom nodded. "His big brother, Burt, is mean, too. Just tell Mikey that if he does it again, you'll knock his head off."

"He'll just laugh," I said, wiping the tears off my face.

Tom pounded one fist into his open hand. "Well, then, tell him that *I'll* knock his head off. I've had plenty of practice."

I looked at Tom. "Gee, thanks," I said. I had never really thought about it, but Tom had the same last name as me. I guess he'd been teased, too.

"Why didn't Mom and Dad change their name?" I asked. "We could be the Harpers or the Smiths, or anything nice and easy."

Tom shrugged. "I asked them once, and they said they had thought about it, but they had never gotten around to it. I know one thing: I'm going to change it as soon as I'm old enough. I'm going to be Tom Jones."

"That's a nice name."

"You're not kidding," Tom said. "It's a nice normal name just for me."

We were both quiet for a few minutes. "Er, Tom," I asked, breaking the silence. "What are you doing in my room?"

"Oh, I came to check on Bobo," Tom said. "Mom said he's sick."

I shook my head. "He's not sick. He's just old, that's all."

Bobo lifted his head from my bed. His eyes were wet, like he'd been crying. Something else was wrong with Bobo, too. I just couldn't figure out what.

8

Tom and Bobo

"He doesn't look so good," Tom said, gently rubbing Bobo's head.

Sure, Bobo's eyes were watery, but so were mine. "Bobo looks great!" I snapped. "There's nothing wrong with him."

Tom shook his head and reached for Bobo. "I'd better have a look at him. Come here, boy."

"No!" I said, pushing Tom's hand away. "I had him first."

Tom didn't pay any attention. He just grabbed Bobo and turned toward the door.

"Mom!" I screamed. "I had Bobo first. MOM!"

Mom leaned against my door frame. "What are you guys fighting over now?"

"He's taking Bobo away," I complained.

"She's already had him for a while," Tom said. "I just want to make sure he's okay. Besides, it's my turn."

"I wasn't done yet!" I snapped.

Mom sighed. "You're done now. Give Tom a turn. I can't believe you two are fighting over Bobo. He's sick, and you're playing tug-of-war with him."

My face turned red and I yelled, "He's not sick! Anyway, Tom started it. I was minding my own business and he came right into my room."

"See if I ever try to help you again," Tom snapped back. I felt bad. After all, Tom *had* offered to help me out with Mikey. I put my head down on the bed. My bad day was getting worse by the second.

Mom frowned at me. "And don't you ever yell at me, young lady. It's time to do your homework," she said as she walked off down the hallway.

Tom smiled at me in his most annoying "I won and you didn't" way. He just took my dog away and slammed the door behind him. Before he left, Bobo looked at me with the saddest eyes I'd ever seen. He knew how much I needed him. What could Tom need Bobo for? Tom didn't have any problems, did he? I bet Tom's best friend and teacher didn't desert him.

I grabbed my backpack from the floor and pulled it onto my lap. "If Miss Snotgrass is such a great teacher, then why did she give us homework on her very first day?" I mumbled to myself. "I bet Amanda couldn't answer *that* question." I felt like calling Amanda on the phone and asking her, but I didn't. Mom would get even madder at me. I read our homework assignment out of my notebook. *Write about the perfect school.* I smiled.

Quickly, I grabbed a pencil and paper. I would tell Miss Snotgrass, Amanda, Carey Armstrong, and the whole world exactly what the best school in the universe would be like. None of them would be a part of it, that's for sure.

9

Bus Stop

The next morning, Amanda gave me a big hug when I walked up to the bus stop. "I'm so sorry," she said.

"It's okay," I said, even though it wasn't. She had been a traitor to Mrs. Holiday and a traitor to me. It would be hard to forgive her, but the hug sure helped.

"I got to the bus stop early and I saw Tom walking to school. He told me about Bobo," Amanda said. She had tears in her eyes.

"Bobo?" I asked. What were we talking about here? I thought Amanda had just

apologized for being mean to me, but that wasn't the case at all.

"I can't believe he's dying," Amanda said. "You've had him since you were a baby. I remember when he used to lick our ice-cream cones."

I shook my head and yelled, "I don't know what you're talking about! Bobo is *not* dying. He's not even sick!"

All the other kids at the bus stop turned around and stared at me. I didn't care. What kind of rotten friend was Amanda, anyway? Why would she say that Bobo was dying?

Carey Armstrong walked up to Amanda and patted her on the shoulder. I had never liked Carey much, and now I knew why. She was a friend-stealer. She was stealing Amanda away from me.

I stood at the edge of the sidewalk by myself and waited for the bus. Then a huge crowd of kids gathered around me. This was the last bus stop, so most kids slept later and cut through yards to catch the bus here. I didn't care about the kids, but I thought about Bobo. He hadn't sat next to me at breakfast like he usually did, waiting for a piece of bacon to fall off my plate. In fact, I hadn't seen Bobo at all this morning. The thought gave me a yucky feeling in the pit of my stomach. I was all set to run back home and check on Bobo when someone tapped me on the shoulder. It was the last person I felt like seeing.

"Hey, Butter-butt!" Mikey teased. "Look out for cars, or you'll be creamed butt in the middle of the highway." For some reason, Mikey and a couple of other boys thought that was so funny. They threw back their heads and laughed in the evil way only boys can. Usually, Amanda snapped at Mikey to make him quit teasing me, but she had her back turned to me this time. I didn't even know if she heard him. Carey's face was so close to hers, it was a wonder they could breathe.

"Do you know how Bridgett can see the future?" Mikey asked his buddies.

A couple of kids shrugged and waited for Mikey to answer. "Her crystal butt!" he cried. All the boys cracked up, which just made Mikey keep going.

"Does anyone know Bridgett's favorite sport?" Mikey said. I tried to ignore him, but my eyes felt all watery. Thankfully, the bus pulled up and I got in line.

Mikey yelled the answer as I stepped on the bus. "Butt-ball! Bridgett likes to play butt-ball!"

10

School

Things were bad. They had never been so bad. All day, I just wanted to go home. I felt my forehead. No fever. The nurse wouldn't let me go home without a fever. Why was it that when you wanted to be sick, you couldn't be?

I tried to pay attention to what we were doing in class. "That's right," Miss Snotgrass was telling Amanda. She'd answered a history question correctly. Amanda flashed her proud smile around the room.

Carey scooted her chair closer and gave Amanda a high five.

I groaned and put my head down on my desk. Maybe, just maybe, everyone would leave me alone for the rest of the day. With my eyes closed, Miss Snotgrass and the rest of the class sounded like bees buzzing around. The next thing I knew, all the kids were rushing out of the room for recess. I stood up slowly and headed for the door, too.

"Bridgett," Miss Snotgrass said. When that didn't stop me, she called out, "Bridgett Butt!"

I stopped dead in my tracks. What did this horrible teacher want now? "Yes, Miss SNOTgrass?" I asked, saying the "snot" part of her name extra loudly.

"I'd like to talk to you for a moment," she said.

Uh-oh. This was definitely not good. I slowly walked over to her desk and stood with my head down. All I could see of

Miss Snotgrass were her ugly bright green shoes. Snot-colored shoes. I almost giggled out loud at the thought.

"Bridgett, I read your paper about the perfect school," Miss Snotgrass said quietly. I clenched my fists together in a knot and wondered what Miss Snotgrass would do to me. Would she send me to the principal's office? I had only written the truth. Can you get in trouble for writing the truth?

"I'm sorry that you are so sad that Mrs. Holiday left," Miss Snotgrass continued. "I hope, in time, you will come to like me a bit."

I didn't say anything, but I knew that would never happen. Miss Snotgrass lifted my paper from her desk and I saw the grade, a B. That wasn't so bad. "You wrote that, in the perfect school, no one teases anyone else about their name. Has anyone ever teased you?" Miss Snotgrass asked.

I looked at her like she was a kangaroo. I knew she wasn't as smart as Mrs.

Holiday, but I didn't think Miss Snotgrass was stupid. My last name was Butt. Did she really think no one had ever teased me? But I didn't feel like explaining it to her. I just shrugged my shoulders.

Miss Snotgrass handed me my paper and said, "If anyone ever teases you, please come tell me. I know a thing or two about being teased."

I nodded. With a name like Snotgrass, I figured she had been teased. But that didn't mean I would ever ask her for help.

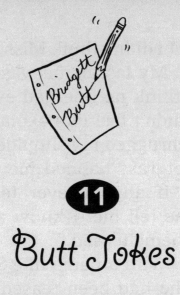

11

Butt Jokes

"Know any good butt jokes?" Mikey asked me at recess. He didn't give me a chance to answer before he went on. "Oh, I forgot," he snickered. "You *are* a butt joke!"

I tried to walk away from Mikey, but he kept following me. Two other boys from class followed, too. They weren't mean like Mikey, but I guess they were bored. Watching me get picked on must have been pretty exciting. This really would have been a good time for some bubble gum. I chewed my lip instead and turned my back to the boys.

"What do you call Bridgett's haircut?" Mikey asked his friends.

"A butt-do," Jason Eddy said with a laugh.

That really cracked the guys up, and they rolled on the ground laughing. Luckily, that gave me a chance to walk away. I saw Amanda and Carey on the monkey bars together. If you ask me, Carey looked a lot like a monkey. They didn't look my way, even when Mikey and his friends swarmed around me. I knew I couldn't count on Amanda to make Mikey leave me alone anymore. My eyes stung with tears, and it wasn't because of Mikey's nasty comments.

"What did Miss SNOTgrass want to talk to you about?" Mikey asked.

"None of your business," I snapped, and hopped on an empty swing.

"It was because you're the teacher's pet, right?" Mikey teased.

I almost laughed, because that was so dumb. I would never be Miss Snotgrass's favorite.

"Miss Snotgrass likes her best because they both have silly names," Chuck Bell said.

"That's true," Mikey said. "What kind of name is Snotgrass, anyway? SNO-O-O-OTGRA-A-AS!"

Mikey kept saying the name over and over. He said the "snotty" part really loud, just like I had earlier. It made me feel bad that I had said it like Mikey had. Finally, I couldn't stand it any longer. When Mikey said "SNO-O-O-OTGRA-A-AS!" again, I jumped off the swing and landed right beside him.

"Listen here, you little jerk," I yelled, and held up my fist in his face. "If you don't shut up, I'm going to knock all the snot out of that runty little nose of yours. You got it?"

Mikey, Chuck, and Jason stood with their mouths wide open. I was pretty shocked myself. Great—now all three of them would probably beat me up. But that didn't happen.

Mikey just shrugged his shoulders. He even looked a little embarrassed. Before he and his friends walked away, he mumbled, "Calm down, Bridgett. We were just having a little fun."

"Fun?" I screamed at his back. "Teasing people is NOT fun! Miss Snotgrass isn't so bad, and it's not fair to make fun of her just because she has a silly name! Why don't you learn how to have fun without being so mean?"

When I stopped yelling, I noticed that everyone on the playground was staring at me. Including Amanda.

12

Amanda in the Middle

"You really told Mikey today at recess," Amanda said from behind me as we were waiting to get on the bus to go home.

I jumped because I hadn't expected her to talk to me. I was even more surprised when Carey spoke up. "That Mikey is just plain mean. I think he needs a good kick in the pants."

"And Bridgett is just the one to give it to him," Amanda said with a giggle. I couldn't figure out if Amanda and Carey were making fun of my last name, or if they were trying to be nice.

Amanda got right to the point. "Why are you so mad at me?" she asked.

"Me?" I asked. "But I thought you hated me."

Amanda shrugged. "You were the one who walked away from me at recess yesterday."

She did have a point. I guess I *had* started the whole mad business. "But you didn't talk to me at all on the bus yesterday afternoon," I said.

"Well, I guess I was a little bit mad at you for leaving me alone on the playground," she told me. "But I'm not mad anymore."

"Why don't you sit with us on the bus today?" Carey suggested.

I chewed my lip. I wanted to sit with Amanda, but I wasn't so sure about Carey. Wasn't she a friend-stealer?

"Come on," Amanda said. "It'll be fun. We'll be like the Three Musketeers."

"Who?" I asked.

"Like the three Powerpuff Girls . . . the

56

Three Bears . . . the Three Little Pigs," Carey added.

We all giggled at the thought of three little pigs sitting on the bus. "Sitting with us sure beats sitting with Mikey," Amanda said.

I had to admit, she was right about that. Sitting with a rabid pit bull would be better than sitting with Mikey again. "Okay," I agreed.

So we all sat down on the bus, with Amanda in the middle. It was a little squished, but not too bad. We stared our meanest stares as Mikey walked down the aisle toward us. He opened his mouth like he wanted to say something to me, but then he just shook his head and headed to the back of the bus.

Amanda, Carey, and I put our heads together and giggled. "He didn't have the nerve to tease you this time," Amanda said.

"You know," Carey said, turning and

looking over the back of the seat, "Mikey is kind of cute."

"Mikey?" I squealed, and we all cracked up laughing.

Amanda was right—it *was* a lot of fun to sit together. Almost as much fun as when Amanda and I used to sit alone.

13

Bobo

It had been fun on the bus with Amanda and Carey, but the minute I stepped onto the sidewalk, things changed. I got scared and worried. What about Bobo? Was he really dying, like Amanda and Tom had said?

The thought made me start running. Suddenly, nothing mattered but Bobo. "Please let him be okay," I said out loud. I even crossed my fingers.

By the time I got home, sweat was pouring down my face. I jerked open the door and screamed, "Bobo!"

Nothing. No barking, not even a whimper.

"Bobo, where are you?" I called. Tears joined the sweat on my face, and I ran around the house, looking in all of Bobo's favorite sleeping spots. He wasn't anywhere.

Tom met me in the kitchen. "You want some milk?" he asked, pouring himself a big glass. Something was definitely wrong. Tom never offered to get me anything.

"I want Bobo," I told him, wiping the tears off my cheeks. "Where is he?"

Tom put the milk back in the refrigerator before answering. "He's gone."

"Gone?" I yelled.

Tom nodded. "Mom took him to the vet."

"But he's going to be all right, isn't he?" I asked.

Tom's eyes looked a little red. Had my big, strong brother been crying? "I don't know," he said with a shrug.

"He will be!" I yelled and threw my backpack on the floor. I ran up to my room and grabbed Bobo's picture off my dresser.

"Please be okay!" I begged Bobo's picture. "What would I do without you?" I sat down on my bed and remembered how Bobo used to chase the ball around the backyard. He had even played soccer with me. I would kick the ball, and he'd try to grab it with his mouth. It had been a long time since Bobo had been so playful.

Tom stopped in my doorway and said exactly what I'd been thinking. "Bobo is getting old."

I nodded, but I kept my mouth closed. I didn't want to start bawling.

Tom sat down on the bed next to me and started to say something, but didn't finish. We both heard the garage door opening at the same time. "Mom's home!" I shouted. We raced downstairs. Tom even let me go first. I had my fingers crossed the whole time.

"Hey, kids," Mom said wearily as she opened the door.

"Mom, where's Bobo?" I asked.

At that exact second, Bobo nudged his way past Mom's leg and into the kitchen.

"Bobo!" Tom yelled.

Tom and I dropped to the floor and started hugging Bobo. Mom laughed and tossed her keys on the counter.

"How come I never get a welcome like that?" she asked.

"Sorry, Mom," I said, giving her a quick hug before going back to pet Bobo.

"So is he okay?" Tom asked.

Mom shook her head. "Not exactly. He's getting really old. I don't know how many more years we'll have Bobo with us."

"But he's all right for now?" I asked.

Mom nodded. "He has an infection, which is why he's been extra sleepy lately. The doctor gave me some pills that should get him fixed up."

Right then, the world was a wonderful place. I didn't even care that my last name

was Butt, or that I had a new teacher named Miss Snotgrass. Bobo licked me on the nose and I knew that sometimes things change. Sometimes the changes are for the better, and sometimes they are for the worse. I was just glad that, for right now, some things had stayed the same, too.

About the Author

Debbie Dadey is the author and co-author of over one hundred twenty-five books, including *Slime Wars* and *Slime Time*, which she wrote with her oldest son, Nathan. In fact, some of the ideas in *The Worst Name in Third Grade* came from her children, too.

Nathan does like weird science fiction shows on TV, and Debbie's daughter, Becky, can't stand them. Her son Alex went to a school where they had a nature area on the playground. The whole family even moved to Texas when Debbie's husband got a new job there. Now she lives in Colorado with her family and two dogs.

Before Debbie was married, her name was Debbie Gibson. It was so easy and common that no one had trouble saying it. One girl in her high school even had the exact same first and last name. Debbie always thought it would be cool to have an unusual name. Now that her last name is Dadey, she's not so sure. People say it wrong a lot. (It's pronounced Day-dee.) She hopes you give kids a break when they have funny names, even if it is a name like Butt!

More books by Debbie Dadey!

The new kid in third grade is weird! He can't remember where he lives, he gobbles up cheeseburgers like he's never seen them before, and oh, yeah, he has gills.

Jake's not sure why he changed from a swamp monster to a kid. But now he's wearing sneakers and dodging bullies in the hallway. Jake wants to be his scary self again—he just doesn't want to morph into a monster in the middle of class!

Boys vs. girls. That's the way it is on Daleside Drive. Slime battles, water balloon fights, practical jokes — it's the same every summer. Until now.

Justin and his friends want to play the coolest game show on TV — *The Slime Wars*. The winners get brand-new bikes and money, money, *money*! The losers get dumped into a gigantic pit of slime.

But the boys have one BIG problem: The girls. Each team needs boys *and* girls. Now, the kids of Daleside Drive have to work together — or they'll all get slimed! Let the Slime Wars begin!